W9-CUG-991

03

BEATRIX POTTER

LETTERS TO CHILDREN

HARVARD COLLEGE LIBRARY

Department of Printing and Graphic Arts

AND

Walker and Company

NEW YORK · 1966

FOREWORD

IT seems impossible that Beatrix Potter was born as long ago as a hundred years, because she only died in 1943. Nearly all adults of today were already born by then, and few indeed of the "properly brought up" English-speaking ones had failed to be given her books as presents when they were children. To read these "Tales" at the right age was to love them—and their inimitable pictures. This monograph is intended as a tribute to celebrate the centenary by one who loved them very much indeed!

Here are reproduced for the first time in facsimile nine letters, owned by the writer of this foreword, which were written by Miss Potter to her young friends Noël, Eric and Freda (sometimes also spelled Frida) Moore. All three were children of her former governess, who lived not far from Bolton Gardens, the author-artist's London home, at Wandsworth, south of the Thames. To be sure, more letters of this same sort, with pictures, exist, but they are jealously guarded by their owners. Very few of them indeed have ever been reproduced.

The earliest the writer has seen is the superb one of eight pages addressed to Noël Moore, and dated September 4th, 1893. It appears in Margaret Lane's excellent biography *The Tale of Beatrix Potter*, London, Frederick Warne and Co., 1946, where the reader also learns that Miss Potter actually borrowed it back from Noël Moore in order to *copy* its principal features—both episodes in the story and the pen drawings themselves! Clearly, then, the various stories which she eventually published had some of their origins in her letters, which fact makes the publication of the letters really important.

Peter Rabbit first appeared in a very modest booklet, roughly five by four inches, "privately printed" before Christmas in 1901. But it is undated. The copy the writer owns is a presentation one "For Mrs. Carver" signed, and labeled as a Christmas present, in that year. But one drawing that does not occur in either the 1893 letter or the published book, showing Peter Rabbit carrying an *extra* coat over his shoulder, is on page four in the first letter to Freda of this monograph (dated June 14, 1897 and reproduced here on the cover). Miss Potter must have been writing on a very hot day (rare in London) for she says, "My rabbit is so hot he does not know what to do with himself. He has such thick fur, I think he would be more comfortable if he had a little coat which would take off," (sic).

There are other quite pertinent drawings and allusions in these nine letters referring to subsequent books. In the letter to Eric, August 8, 1896, possible prototypes of *Mrs. Tiggy Winkle* (1905) are shown at the top of the first and second pages, a possible prototype of Mr. Brown, in *Squirrel Nutkin* (1903) on page four at the bottom. But closest of all to the *Squirrel Nutkin* illustrations is the drawing on page four of the letter to Noël of August 26, 1897, where all the squirrels are seen paddling their rafts almost exactly as in the illustration on page seventeen in the printed book, except that they are approaching the reader instead of going away!

Other prototypes could be cited here, but two more should suffice to prove the writer's contention that Miss Potter mulled over her ideas and pictures for her stories years in advance. In the letter to Frida (spelt with an "i" this time!) of July 30th,

1898, on page two, a pair of mice are seated at the table very much as they appear in the *Tale of Two Bad Mice*, of 1904, on pages twenty-nine and thirty-two, while the drawing on page one of the letter to Frida, dated January 26th, 1900 is even more akin to the picture of Hunca Munca, with her housemaid's dress and apron, on page eighty-four in this same work.

The last of the nine letters reproduced in this monograph is not illustrated, but it contains very important bibliographical information. Again to Freda (now spelt with an "e"), and dated October 6th, 1902, it states on page three, "The colored edition of *Peter Rabbit* is ready, [and] I think it is to be in the shops this week. . . . The publisher has sold more copies than he printed (6,000) so he is going to print another edition at once." This closely dates the second edition (Frederick Warne and Co.) of *Peter Rabbit*, which otherwise has not even the year of issue on its title. Similarly, this letter tells us (also on page three) that "Your mouse-book is not printed yet." This does not refer to the *Tale of Two Bad Mice* of 1904, but to its predecessor *The Tailor of Gloucester* of 1902 and 1903, which is perhaps the favorite of them all, with its wonderfully subtle phrase, on page eighty (in the 1903 edition), which no one can forget who has read the story: "no more twist" (left as a note by the mice in tiny writing with reference to the unfinished "cherry colored button hole.")

For the convenience of those who find Beatrix Potter's own hand less "readable" than her drawings, each letter has been transcribed in type as accurately as possible.

Cambridge, August, 1966   *Philip Hofer*

My dear Eric,

My little cousin Molly Gaddum has got a squirrel who has 2 baby squirrels in a hay nest. you cannot think how pretty. They are not much bigger than mice yet. They live in a box in the hay loft, & one day

Molly opened the lid and Mrs Squirrel jumped out. They had such a business to catch her. Jim her brother has 2 jack daws which sit all day on a stick in a corner, I think they are not very interesting, he wishes to give me one. He has also got a hedge hog & some gold fish. There are plenty of hedge hogs here in the fields. they come out in the

evening. So do the rabbits, there are
two black ones, in a field near
the house.

Our coachman brought his cat in
a basket. It mewed
dreadfully amongst the
luggage, but I think it is
enjoying itself. It sings songs
with the
gardener's
cat, which is grey, + the farm cat,
which is white with a black tail.
There is a very pretty yellow colley

dog, it is so

clever with the sheep,
it drives them right & left, which
ever way it is told and never
bites them. Sometimes it comes in
at our dining room window & shake
hands. We have got a
tame owl
he eats
mice, he sits with a tail
hanging out of his mouth.
I remain yours aff.
Beatrix Potter

DOBBIN

June 14th 97

BESS DARLING JOAN APRIL

My dear Freda,

I think I must write you a letter too. What a nice time you are having, going to so many tea parties!

I wonder if there are going to [be]
any decorations at Wandsworth o[n]
Jubilee Day. I shall not go [to]
see the procession; it is too hot.

I shall stop at home and ha[ve]
a large flag out of
the window —
At the last
Jubilee there was a
wind, and our flag
kept rolling up.

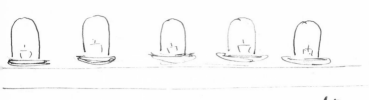

We had to reach out of the
window with a broom to unroll
it. We are going to have night lights
on the window sills, red, blue, and
white.

My rabbit is so hot he does
not know what to do with
himself. He has such thick

fur, I think he would be
more comfortable if he had

a little coat which would take

off. I shall send this to

Wandsworth, I daresay it will be sent

on to Ipswich, if you have not

come home. I remain

yours affectionately

Beatrix Potter,

The little foal belongs to my uncle, it is so
tame.

My dear Noël,

We have got a trap for
catching minnows, which is
amusing.

It is made
of perforated zinc. I did not
believe it would answer, but my
brother tied a bit of string to it,
put some bread inside and
watched. The minnows

came all round snuffing and at
last one old fish found the wa[y]
in at the end, and all the othe[r]
followed. I should think there w[ere]
50 or 60 inside when it was pull[ed]
out of the water.   We use them
for bait for larger fish, trout
and perch.   The fishing is not
very good in the lake; the groom,
who drives my pony, catches more
than anybody.
He is always at it. One day th[e]
otter hounds came round the lake

to hunt; they did not find an
otter and we have never seen one,
as they only come out at
night. I went out in our boat
& watched the
dogs. The men
wade about with long poles.
There is a lady who lives on an
island on the lake who told us
some curious things about animals
swimming. She had a cat which
she did not want, so she gave
it to some one in Keswick, but a

week afterwards it came back into her house dripping wet!

Also when her nuts are ripe, squirrels appear on the island, but she has not seen them coming. There is an American story that squirrels go down the rivers on little rafts, using their tails

for sails, but I think the Keswick squirrels must swim. I must write to Eric next time I hope you are quite well again. I remain dear Noel yrs aff —

Beatrix Potter.

Harescombe Grange.
Nov 3ᵘ 97

My dear Frida,

I must tell you a funny thing about the guinea-hens here. You know what they are like, I daresay, grey speckled birds with very small silly heads. One day Parton, the coachman, saw them in the field, running backwards and forwards, bobbing their heads up (They say Pot Rack! Pot Rack! Pot Rackety Rack!) & down & cackling. They were watching something white, which was waving about in the long grass. Parton could not tell what it was either, so he went close up to it, & up jumped a

fox! It had been lying on its back
waving its tail.

I heard of another fox when I was a
Woodcote, which had gone to the
gamekeeper's & killed 4 hens & then
went to sleep in
the pig stye with
the pig. The
gamekeeper was so cross, he said the
people who had the foxhounds had let
loose some tame foxes, & they would not
stay in the woods. He ran for a gun but
Mr Fox woke up.
yrs aff.
Beatrix Potter.

July 30ᵗʰ 98

My dear Frida,

I am writing to you instead of Eric because I think you saw my tame snail, and he did not see it. I will write to him and Marjory next time. I had to dig up my snails' nest when I left home. I found there were 79 large eggs!

It was such a quee

nest in the ground

and the snail had covered it up

with soil. The eggs were white

just like the

eggs you

had for breakfast,

They would be just

the right size for little mice!

I brought them here in a lit

box; the old snail did not ta

any more trouble about them af

she had covered up the hole.
Yesterday morning, after 4 weeks,
the eggs began to hatch,
4 came out, and 4 more today.

They are such pretty little snails
with quite hard shells, but almost
like glass, I expect they will
soon go darker, they are
beginning to eat.
My brother has got
a jack daw, a
very sly bird

Directly we let him loose he gets into the fire place and brings out rubbish which has been thrown in the fender I think he must have lived in a chimney, it will be very awkward when the fire is lighted. We are all quite well and there has not been quite so much rain as there usually is here, but I shall be glad to get home again, I don't like going away for such a long time I remain yrs affectionately

Beatrix Potter.

16 Robertson Terrace
Hastings Jan 13" 99.

My dear Frida,

It is very wet today but there is something to look at, just opposite the house. The sea has knocked over 20 yards of iron railing and thrown great big coping stones onto the road. It happened in the night, but I saw very fine waves yesterday. I stood on the end of the terrace

and looked down on a lower
street where the water was
rushing down the gutter.
People were putting boards over
the windows but it flooded
a boot shop in the night.
I'm afraid I cannot draw it
but I tried to take some
photographs of the little boys
rushing up the lamp posts &
railings. There was a large crowd
& whenever anyone tried to get
round the corner of the terrace

they made such a noise, one old gentleman was wet all over, and some girls came round when it was a little quieter & found themselves in a pond. There were baskets & things floating about, and a very nice brown terrier dog, barking & rushing about. A

stupid boy threw a stone into
the waves & it jumped off the
wall before any one could stop it
I thought it would be drowned
but the next big waves threw
it out again into the road. It
walked off looking quite
offended but I
think it was

rather frightened. The sea has
smashed a large gas lamp at the
pier, I hope nothing worse. The Hastings
boats all came home in a great hurry
before the gale. I hope you are all
very well, yrs aff.
Beatrix Potter.

Derwent Cottage
Winchelsea
Jan 26th 1900.

My dear Frida,

I am staying in such
a funny old cottage; it is
like the little mouse-houses I
have often drawn in pictures.
I am sure_(when I am half
asleep)_that it is a mouse-house
for Mrs Cooke,
the landlady,
and her family
go to bed up a sort of

ladder stair-case, and I can
hear them scuffling about
upon the rafters just above
my head! The ceiling of
my bed-room is so low I
can touch it with my
hand. and there is a little

attic window
just the
right size
for mice to

peep out of.   Then there are

cupboards in the walls, that

little people could hide in,

and

steps

up and

down

to

the rooms, and doors in every

corner; very draughty!   I wish

it would stop raining and b
bright and fine; I don't th
my brother + I will stop mo
than a week if the weather do
not mend. We came here las
Wednesday. I have been for 2
long walks, it is pretty country, +
on nearly
every hill there is
a windmill, spinning round
in the wind and rain.
I am dear Frida yrs affectionate
Beatrix Potter.

April 24ᵗʰ Tenby '00

My dear Frida,

I went a long way in a boat one day to see puffins who live on an island. They are black & white birds with very large red bills. They are considered very silly, and look something like parrots that have tumbled into the water, but they behave in a very sly way. They never take the trouble to build nests, but live in rabbit holes

They look for a nice hole and
drive the rabbits out. They do

not live here in the winter but
arrived about a fortnight since, it
must be most annoying to the
rabbits to see them landing. There
are little rabbits by this time, lots
of them, all
comfortable in
bed, I am
sure they
don't give up

their holes without a fight!

I don't believe either rabbits or
puffins are able to hurt much,
but the puffins always win and
take possession of the best holes.
I don't know what

becomes of the rabbits; perhaps they
go and live with the jackdaws, who
are much more polite, They walk about

bobbing their heads as if they were bowing. I notice the rabbits & jackd[aws] live close togeth[er] quite nicely.

The jackdaws go into holes in the rock exactly like little square doors. I am very sleepy with going on the sea in the wind. With love to all of you from yrs aff—

Beatrix Potter.

Miss Potter is sitting upon her book at present & considering! The publisher cannot tell what has become of it.

Oct 6th 02

My dear Freda,

I had such nice letters from you and Marjory just after I came here, and I have been intending to answer them all Summer, but I have left it till the last day! We are coming home on Wednesday, we have all got colds in our noses at present to end up with. I hope I shall be able

to drive over to see your
Mamma with the new pony;
but I shall not keep him long
he does not improve his
manners when he gets to dend
One of his little games — when
he is lazy and does not want
to go — is to sail away round
a corner ↗ up a wrong road.
Then I pull ↗ scold; ↗ then the
groom takes the reins ↗ pulls, ↗
at last we stop — ↗ then the groom
gets out ↗ turns him round and
punches him very hard in the ribs
Other times he stands still at the

ttom of a hill & won't go at all.
When he does occasionally go, he
a very good pony indeed & nice
looking. Your mouse-book is not
printed yet; but the coloured
edition of Peter Rabbit is ready, &
I think it is to be in the shops
this week; if there are any
book shops about Wandsworth you
must look whether it is in the
windows. The publisher has sold
more copies than he printed (6000)
so he is going to print another
edition at once. We have had
a very cold summer, the last

few weeks have been the pleasantest
we have had; although it is sharp
& frosty there is less wind & more
sunshine than in August. My brother
has been shooting pheasants & rabbits
lots of rabbits; the gardener puts a
ferret into the hole & then the rabbit
rushes out; he got 11 today. I have
a little rabbit which I tamed, it
jumps over my hands for bits of biscuit,
but it is so frightened of every one else
I cannot show off its tricks to people.
My brother was bitten with a snake a
fortnight ago, he had a bad arm but
it is all right again now. We have
caught a good many pike in the lake, we
fish with a thing they call a "wag tail"!
It is a very ugly imitation fish made of
bits of leather. I must do some more
packing, so good night. & love to all of
you, from yrs aff

Beatrix Potter

TRANSCRIPTION OF LETTERS

Aug 8th 96.
Lakefield,
Sawrey,
My dear Eric,   Ambleside.

My little cousin Molly Gaddum has got a squirrel who has
2 baby squirrels in a hay nest, you cannot think how pretty.
They are not much bigger than mice yet. They live in a box in
the hay loft, & one day Molly opened the lid and Mrs Squirrel
jumped out. They had such a business to catch her. Jim her
brother has 2 jackdaws which sit all day on a stick in a corner,
I think they are not very interesting, he wishes to give me one.
He has also got a hedge hog & some gold fish. There are plenty
of hedge hogs here in the fields, they come out in the evening.
So do the rabbits, there are two black ones in a field near the
house. Our coachman brought his cat in a basket. It mewed
dreadfully amongst the luggage, but I think it is enjoying
itself. It sings songs with the gardener's cat, which is grey, &
the farm cat, which is white with a black tail. There is a very
pretty yellow colley dog, it is so clever with the sheep, it
drives them right & left, which ever way it is told and never
bites them. Sometimes it comes in at our dining room window
& shakes hands. We have got a tame owl he eats mice, he sits
with a tail hanging out of his mouth.

I remain yours aff.

Beatrix Potter

June 14th 97
2, Bolton Gardens, S.W.

My dear Freda,

I think I must write you a letter too. What a nice time you are having, going to so many tea parties! I wonder if there are going to be any decorations at Wandsworth on Jubilee Day. I shall not go to see the procession; it is too hot.

I shall stop at home and have a large flag out of the window. At the last Jubilee there was a wind, and our flag kept rolling up. We had to reach out of the window with a broom to unroll it. We are going to have night lights on the window sills, red, blue, and white. My rabbit is so hot he does not know what to do with himself. He has such thick fur, I think he would be more comfortable if he had a little coat which would take off. I shall send this to Wandsworth. I daresay it will be sent on to Ipswich, if you have not come home. I remain yours affectionately

Beatrix Potter

The little foal belongs to my uncle, it is so tame.

August 26th 97
Lingholm, Keswick,
Cumberland

My dear Noël,

We have got a trap for catching minnows, which is amusing. It is made of perforated zinc. I did not believe it would answer, but my brother tied a bit of string to it, put some bread inside and watched. The minnows came all round snuffing and at last one old fish found the way in at the end, and all the others followed. I should think there were 50 or 60 inside when it was pulled out of the water. We use them for bait for larger fish, trout and perch. The fishing is not very good in the lake; the groom, who drives my pony, catches more than anybody. He is always at it. One day the otter hounds came round the lake to hunt, they did not find an otter and we have never seen one, as they only come out at night. I went out in our boat and watched the dogs. The men wade about with long poles. There is a lady who lives on an island on the lake who told me some curious things about animals swimming. She had a cat which she did not want, so she gave it to someone in Keswick, but a week afterwards it came back into her house dripping wet! Also when her nuts are ripe, squirrels appear on the island, but she has not seen them coming. There is an American story that squirrels go down the rivers on little rafts, using their tails for sails, but I think the Keswick squirrels must swim. I must write to Eric next time. I hope you are quite well again. I remain dear Noël yrs aff—

Beatrix Potter.

Harescombe Grange.
Nov 3rd 97

My dear Frida,

I must tell you a funny thing about the guinea-hens here. You know what they are like, I daresay, grey speckled birds with very small silly heads. One day Parton, the coachman, saw them in the field, running backwards and forwards, bobbing their heads up & down & cackling. (They say Pot Rack! Pot Rack! Pot Rackety Rack!) They were watching something white, which was waving about in the long grass. Parton could not tell what it was either, so he went close up to it & up

43

jumped a fox! It had been lying on its back waving its tail. I heard of another fox when I was at Woodcote, which had gone to the gamekeeper's & killed 4 hens & then went to sleep in the pig stye with the pig. The gamekeeper was so cross, he said the people who had the foxhounds had let loose some tame foxes, & they would not stay in the woods. He ran for a gun but Mr. Fox woke up.

Yrs aff.

Beatrix Potter.

July 30th 98
Lingholm, Keswick, Cumberland.

My dear Frida,

I am writing to you instead of Eric because I think you saw my tame snail, and he did not see it. I will write to him and Marjory next time. I had to dig up my snail's nest when I left home. I found there were 79 large eggs! It was such a queer nest in the ground and the snail had covered it up with soil. The eggs were white just like the eggs you had for breakfast, they would be just the right size for little mice! I brought them here in a little box; the old snail did not take any more trouble about them after she had covered up the hole. Yesterday morning, after 4 weeks, the eggs began to hatch, 9 came out, and 4 more today. They are such pretty little snails with quite hard shells, but almost like glass, I expect they will soon go darker, they are beginning to eat.

My brother has got a jackdaw, a very sly bird. Directly we let him loose he gets into the fire place and brings out rubbish which has been thrown in the fender. I think he must have lived in a chimny, it will be very awkward when the fire is

lighted. We are all quite well and there has not been quite so much rain, as there usually is here, but I shall be glad to get home again, I don't like going away for such a long time.
I remain yrs affectionately
      Beatrix Potter.

---

16 Robertson Terrace
Hastings Jan 13th 99

My dear Frida,

It is very wet today but there is something to look at, just opposite the house. The sea has knocked over 20 yards of iron railing and thrown great big coping stones onto the road. It happened in the night, but I saw very fine waves yesterday. I stood on the end of the terrace and looked down on a lower street where the water was rushing down the gutter. People were putting boards over the windows but it flooded a boot-shop in the night. I'm afraid I cannot draw it but I tried to take some photographs of the little boys rushing up the lamp posts & railings. There was a large crowd & whenever anyone tried to get round the corner of the terrace they made such a noise, one old gentleman was wet all over, and some girls came round when it was a little quieter & found themselves in a pond. There were baskets & things floating about, and a very nice brown terrier dog, barking & rushing about. A stupid boy threw a stone into the waves & it jumped off the wall before anyone could stop it, I thought it would be drowned but the next big waves threw it out again into the road. It walked off looking quite offended but I think it was rather frightened. The sea has smashed a large gas lamp at the pier, I hope nothing worse. The Hastings boats all came home in a great hurry before the gale. I hope you are all very well, yrs aff.
      Beatrix Potter.

Durwent Cottage
Winchelsea
Jan 26th 1900.

My dear Frida,

I am staying in such a funny old cottage; it is like the little mouse-houses I have often drawn in pictures. I am sure—(when I am half asleep)—that it is a mouse-house; for Mrs Cooke, the landlady, and her family go to bed up a sort of ladder stair-case, and I can hear them scuffling about upon the rafters just above my head! The ceiling of my bed-room is so low I can touch it with my hand, and there is a little lattice window just the right size for mice to peep out of. Then there are cupboards in the walls, that little people could hide in, and steps up and down into the rooms, and doors in every corner; very draughty! I wish it would stop raining and be bright and fine; I don't think my brother & I will stop more than a week if the weather does not mend. We came here last Wednesday. I have been for 2 long walks, it is pretty country, & on nearly every hill there is a windmill, spinning round in the wind and rain.

I am dear Frida yrs affectionately
Beatrix Potter.

Tenby
April 24th 00

My dear Frida,

I went a long way in a boat one day to see puffins who live on an island. They are black & white birds with very large red bills. They are considered very silly, and look something like parrots that have tumbled into the water, but they behave in a

46

very sly way. They never take the trouble to build nests, but live in rabbit holes, they look for a nice hole and drive the rabbits out. They do not live here in the winter but arrived about a fortnight since, it must be most annoying to the rabbits to see them landing. There are little rabbits by this time lots of them, all comfortable in bed, I am sure they don't give up their holes without a fight! I don't believe either rabbits or puffins are able to hurt much, but the puffins always win and take possession of the best holes. I don't know what becomes of the rabbits; perhaps they go and live with the jackdaws, who are much more polite, they walk about bobbing their heads as if they were bowing. I notice the rabbits & jackdaws live close together quite nicely. The jackdaws go into holes in the rock exactly like little square doors. I am very sleepy with going on the sea in the wind. With love to all of you from yrs aff.

Beatrix Potter

Miss Potter is sitting upon her book at present & considering! The publisher cannot tell what has become of it.

Oct 6th 02
Eeswyke,
Sawrey,
Lancashire

My dear Freda,

I had such nice letters from you and Marjory just after I came here, and I have been intending to answer them all summer, but I have left it till the last day! We are coming home on Wednesday. We have all got colds in our noses at present to end up with. I hope I shall be able to drive over to see your

Mamma with the new pony; but I shall not keep him long if he does not improve his manners when he gets to London. One of his little games—when he is lazy and does not want to go—is to sail away round a corner & up a wrong road. Then I pull & scold & then the groom takes the reins & pulls, & at last we stop, & then the groom gets out & turns him round and punches him very hard in the ribs! Other times he stands still at the bottom of a hill & won't go at all. When he does occasionally go, he is a very good pony indeed & nice looking. Your mouse-book is not printed yet; but the coloured edition of Peter Rabbit is ready, & I think it is to be in the shops this week; if there are any book shops about Wandsworth you must look whether it is in the windows. The publisher has sold more copies than he printed (6000) so he is going to print another edition at once. We have had a very cold summer, the last few weeks have been the pleasantest we have had; although it is sharp & frosty there is less wind & more sunshine than in August. My brother has been shooting pheasants & rabbits, lots of rabbits; the gardener puts a ferret into the hole & then the rabbit rushes out; he got 11 today. I have a little rabbit which I tamed, it jumps over my hands for bits of biscuit, but it is so frightened of everyone else I cannot show off its tricks to people. My brother was bitten with a snake a fortnight ago, he had a bad arm but it is all right again now. We have caught a good many pike in the lake, we fish with a thing they call a "wagtail"! It is a very ugly imitation fish made of bits of leather. I must do some more packing, so good night, & love to all of you, from yrs aff–

Beatrix Potter